DANCING TOM

By Elizabeth Coatsworth

DANCING TOM

By ELIZABETH COATSWORTH
Pictures by GRACE PAULL

NEW YORK — THE MACMILLAN COMPANY — 1944

PRINTED IN THE UNITED STATES OF AMERICA
NORWOOD PRESS—NORWOOD, MASS., U.S.A.

To Carpy
who was born in the valley of
the Mississippi, and is as brave
and merry as Jenny herself.

NEARLY a hundred years ago there lived on the upper Ohio a man, a woman and a baby boy. The man's name was Caleb Foster and his wife's name was Jenny. The little boy, who was only a year old, was called John. They lived in a log house which Caleb had built himself, and all about them was the land Caleb had cleared with the help of Lion, the yellow ox, and Tiger, the brindle one.

There he planted corn and beans and rye, but his hay came from the wild meadows near the river. Caleb and Jenny were young and strong. He cut down trees, split fence rails, plowed, hoed, and built, hunted and trapped. She cooked and kept

things clean, spun, wove and dyed the cloth she made, boiled soap, knitted stockings, wove cornhusk mats for the floor, dipped candles, and did a hundred other things.

But busy as they were they had time to be happy.

They were king and queen of their own clearing and John was the prince. Everything they needed they had. When they wanted something they made it.

The few things they could not make Caleb got by trading his furs or Jenny's homespuns.

They had done well. In their shed were Lion and Tiger and Bessie the red and white cow. They had a rooster and ten speckled hens, Millie and Whitey the sheep, Diamond the hound, and someday they hoped to have a pig.

One October day their neighbor, Mrs. Hezekiah Lee, invited Jenny to a quilting bee. Jenny took John and was gone all day. At last Caleb grew worried and went down the road to meet her.

Not far from the cabin he came upon her. She had John under one arm and a poke under the other, and she was pink with effort and laughter.

"I don't know which wiggles most," said Jenny. "Now, what do you think I have in my poke?"

Caleb couldn't guess, so Jenny gave him John to carry and when they got home she emptied out on the floor of the cabin a little fat pig with a black spot on one side and little black hoofs.

"Mrs. Lee gave him to me," she cried. "Their sow had a bigger litter than she could manage. Isn't he a wonderful little pig?"

"He is wonderful," said Caleb. "I'll build him a little pen to-morrow so the bears won't get him. It will certainly be nice to have our own ham and bacon next fall."

Jenny looked at the little pig as though she didn't like the thought that he would ever be ham and bacon.

A few weeks later she said, "Caleb, do come out and see what John and I have taught the little pig to do."

When Jenny came near the pigsty she raised the pail in which she had the slops and began whistling "Yankee Doodle."

Then the little pig got up on his black hind hoofs and danced in time to the whistle.

"I'm teaching him to turn as he dances," said Jenny. "He's the little pig who danced a jig, isn't he, John?"

Caleb and Jenny laughed at the sight and John laughed because they did.

"A pig that can dance should have a name," said Caleb. "Shall we call him Dancing Tom?"

It was not very long after this that a traveler on horseback stopped at the cabin of Caleb and Jenny to spend the night. He was just back from the newly opened lands along the Mississippi, and had wonderful tales to tell of the richness of the country. As soon as he could make arrangements for taking his family, he would go back.

For many days after the stranger's visit Caleb was more silent than usual, thinking of what the man had told them. At last he said one day:

"Jenny, the land here is not so very good after all. If we went farther west it would be better. Would it be all right for you and John?"

Jenny kissed him.

"John and I want to be wherever you want to be," she said.

Next spring, sometimes alone, sometimes with the help of a neighbor, Caleb began building a flat boat. It was broad and strong. Inside could be carried all they had in their cabin and

barn. At the forward end of the deck he built a shed for **Lion** and **Tige**, **Bessie**, the sheep, and **Dancing Tom**. At the stern, near the steering sweep, he built a smaller house for **Jenny** and **John** and himself.

The neighbors came to wave their farewells. Caleb stood at the steering sweep, and two young men who had decided to come with him because they, too, wanted to go West, seized the poles with which to help steer the boat down the current.

Bessie the cow, not liking the new experience, bawled from the shed, and Jennie whistled "Yankee Doodle" to her pig.

The flat boat started its long journey with Dancing Tom doing a little jig on its deck.

Down the river the flat boat traveled for more than a month. On fine days Jenny brought her spinning wheel out on deck and worked. John had a rope around his waist to keep him from falling overboard. All the animals soon grew used to floating down the river, and every evening Tom danced for his supper.

"It seems a pity he's ever got to be bacon and ham," sighed Jenny.

One day as they were nearing a turn in the river someone shot arrows at them from the woods. Jenny snatched up John and ran to shelter. The three men poled with all their might, forcing the heavy boat away from the shore. Then Jenny, who had been loading the gun, shot through the windows of the after-house toward the woods. They saw no one. When they were well beyond the bend they counted five arrows in the deck, but no one had been hurt.

Another time they were caught on a sand bar, and it was not until another boat came along and helped them that they were able to get off.

Still another time they hit so hard on a log hidden under the water that it injured the heavy planking and they had to pull ashore for repairs.

In rainy weather it was dull for the animals and dull for Jenny and John in the little after-house. But on sunny days it was gay on deck. There were so many new things to see.

There were forests, with here and there a clearing; and boats of all kinds passing quickly down the river and slowly, slowly up the river. Sometimes when they tied up near the shore friendly Indians would come to trade with them.

They always very much admired Dancing Tom.

One night an Indian tried to steal Tom, but Diamond heard him and set up such a terrible barking that the Indian ran away.

Whenever he could, Caleb spent the night near where some other flat boat was moored. Then both families felt safe to go ashore and light a fire and talk until the moon was low in the sky.

Sometimes five or six boats would all be moored close together. Someone was sure to bring out a fiddle and then everyone danced. John, safe in some new friend's lap, would watch

Caleb and Jenny dancing with the others. There was no one who could dance them down.

Then sometimes Jenny would show how Tom could dance too. He was more than half grown now, and seemed to enjoy the laughter and hand clapping that greeted his little jig. The fame of Dancing Tom went up and down the river. It seemed a shame that such a clever pig must some day be bacon and ham.

Jenny often talked to Diamond but more often to Tom.

"When we build our new home I'm going to burn that Wandering Foot quilt, which Aunt Sarah gave us when we were married. She called it the Turkey Foot pattern, but I know its real name. Anyone who sleeps under a Wandering Foot quilt has to keep on moving. I like coming down the river but this is far enough. I want John to grow up settled."

Diamond and Dancing Tom always listened carefully to Jenny—especially Dancing Tom.

One day a boat passed them which was painted in bright colors and had its name on the prow and stern—*The Emporium*. It was a store boat, and when Caleb blew on his cow horn it tied up, and he traded for some gingham for Jenny, a new ax-head for himself, and a monkey on a stick for John. Next morning Caleb brought out another surprise for Jenny, a little mirror, so she wouldn't have to do her hair looking down in the pail of water any more.

Where the Ohio joined the Mississippi there was a village of boats. There were house boats and store boats, saloon boats and even a theater boat—all joined together like chips of wood in an eddy. Roosters crowed from the decks, dogs barked, and here and there a cat washed her paws on the roof of a cabin.

There was even a boat where the children went to school. The fame of Dancing Tom had gone before them down the river.

School was closed and all the children ran out on deck with their teacher to watch Tom dance when the Fosters' boat tied up near them.

"Hurrah! hurrah! for Dancing Tom!" they shouted.

Caleb did not stay long in the village of boats—just long enough to ask some questions about land. He decided to go downriver. If he had gone upriver he would have had to hire many boatmen, to pole and haul and drag his boat against the wide yellow waters of the Mississippi. Even going down the river was dangerous. He learned all he could about the bad stretches, and then started out as boldly as ever.

After only a week on the twisting waters of the great river Caleb found land that he liked the looks of. There was a spring on it, and some of the land was open and some was wooded. He and his companions moored the flat boat for the last time and the next day began to take it apart.

First they built, on shore, a cabin of its timbers. Caleb had even brought brick with him for a chimney.

Then they built a barn for Lion and Tige, Bessie, the two sheep and Dancing Tom. For a while the animals lived in very unsheltered quarters on the half-torn-down flat boat, but soon they, too, were ashore with good earth under their hoofs.

How the rooster crowed the first morning on their own land!
The leftover timbers they split for the first fence rails and
Caleb made a doorstep from the blade of the sweep.

"It has steered us for hundreds of miles," he said, "now it
should settle down with us."

Jenny liked the new house. She planted some rose shoots she had brought with her, and hollyhock seeds by the door. Caleb built a fence around her flowers to protect them.

"Tom had better run loose," he said. "There's nothing like a hog for keeping new land clear of snakes."

"Wouldn't a rattler kill him?" asked Jenny. She was very fond of her pig.

"No," said Caleb. "Somehow the poison doesn't go through their fat. Hogs like to eat rattlesnakes about as much as acorns."

So daytimes Dancing Tom ran loose, though still Jenny whistled "Yankee Doodle" for him when she brought out the slops, and still he rose up to his hind feet and danced for her. John was getting big enough to enjoy the game. He would dance too, imitating Tom.

It was a sight that made Jenny laugh and laugh even after the hardest day's work. Caleb laughed too, but he said:

"Tom's growing into a regular hog. Soon it will be time to turn him into bacon and ham."

Then Jenny looked sad.

The weeks went by. The men who had come down the river with them went away on their own adventures. Jenny secretly burned the Wandering Foot quilt. She wanted to stay here always with the huge river at her feet. At first she was afraid that John might fall into it, but soon she could trust him to keep away from the bank. He was a handsome little boy, full of curiosity and courage. Caleb and Jenny thought he was the finest little boy in the world.

One day Jenny was hoeing in the garden near the cabin. It was a day so fine that all the birds were singing. The hens were scratching contentedly in the dust. The cattle and sheep were grazing among the burned-over stumps of the clearing.

By the shed, wandering where he wanted to, was Dancing Tom.

Little John was near her, very earnestly digging a hole in the dirt with an old spoon.

Caleb and Diamond had gone hunting, but Jenny liked to be alone. She was not afraid, and she was not lonely. Only when she looked at Tom she felt sad. She couldn't keep him much longer, she knew.

Just then she noticed that Millie, the black-nosed sheep, seemed to have caught her foot in a hole.

"I don't want her to break a leg," thought Jenny, as she climbed over the fence. She had to go toward Millie very slowly so as not to frighten her and make her jerk her leg.

"Here, Millie, nice Millie," she called, holding out her hand as though there were salt in it.

Millie stared with her gray agate eyes and breathed hard, but at last she let Jenny get near her. The poor leg had been caught between two stones, but Jenny pulled it free safely.

"Mind where you're going, Millie," she said.

She turned back toward her garden. Everything looked so nice from here, the river seen through the trees, and the cabin with unbroken glass in every window. There was John, bless him, not far from where she had left him, and after something as usual. She'd find a ladybug or butterfly in his fat little hand.

It was not until Jenny was climbing the fence again that she knew what John was after. She heard before she saw, heard that rattling like dry peas quickly shaken in a dipper, and then she saw the flat arrow-shaped head above the coils of the rattle-snake.

Jenny was used to acting quickly, but no woman could have reached the snake before John did. As she ran, she called out; but John was too interested to hear her. She saw him take another step and reach out his hand.

Jenny kept on running and calling.

But it was Tom that reached the snake first, grunting with satisfaction. The flat head struck twice at the hog, but then Tom's hoofs came down on its back and broke it. Jenny snatched up John.

"Naughty Tom! Naughty Tom!" screamed John, beating on Jenny's shoulder with his fists. He howled with rage. He had wanted that thing which rattled and Tom had taken it away from him. Jenny cried too, but she cried from joy.

When Caleb and Diamond came home that evening Jenny ran to meet them, holding John tight by the hand.

"I have so much to tell you," she cried. "I don't know where to begin!"

Caleb hung up a fine turkey under the eaves.

"Let's begin with supper then, Jenny," he said. "A hungry man has no ears. After supper, we'll sit on the doorstep and I'll light my pipe to keep away the mosquitoes, and then you can tell me."

Jenny could scarcely bear to keep silence that long, but she managed to serve the venison stew and the corn pones she had cooked in the ashes, the buttermilk and the stirabout pudding.

At last the meal was over and they were sitting side by side on the doorsill of the cabin, their feet upon the sweep blade of the flat boat. Caleb filled his pipe and Jenny ran to get him a coal from the fire in the small tongs, stopping a moment to take another look at John in his cradle by the hearth. Caleb lighted his pipe.

"Now tell me," he said.

When Jenny had told him the story of Millie, and John and the rattlesnake and Tom, Caleb drew a long breath.

"Look, I've saved the rattles," said Jenny.

Caleb counted them. There were eleven.

"A big snake," said Caleb. "Still, even a little one would have been big enough to kill John."

First Caleb went in to see John in his cradle by the hearth. The little boy seemed so full of courage and curiosity, even in his sleep. Caleb stood a long time looking down at his son and Jenny stood beside him, saying nothing.

Then Caleb went out to where Tom was still rooting and grunting in the last of the sunlight. Caleb watched him for quite a while too.

"From now on," he said suddenly, "your name's Dancing Tom Foster."

Dancing Tom paid no attention, but Jenny said quickly, with shining eyes:

"Then he doesn't have to be ham and bacon—ever?"

"Certainly not," said Caleb. "Didn't you hear me say that his name was Foster? From now on he's one of the family."

Then Jenny laughed, and hearing her laugh Caleb laughed too; and at so much laughter Dancing Tom grunted absentmindedly, and getting to his short hind legs danced a rather short jig, for he was growing stout and easily got out of breath.